The Mysterious Cases of
MR. PIN

The Mysterious Cases of
MR. PIN

Vol. I

by Mary Elise Monsell
illustrated by Eileen Christelow

AN AUTHORS GUILD BACKINPRINT.COM EDITION

The Mysterious Cases of MR. PIN
Vol. I

AN AUTHORS GUILD BACKINPRINT.COM EDITION

Published by iUniverse, Inc.

For information address:
iUniverse, Inc.
2021 Pine Lake Road, Suite 100
Lincoln, NE 68512
www.iuniverse.com

Originally published by Atheneum

Because of the dynamic nature of the Internet, any Web addresses
or links contained in this book may have changed
since publication and may no longer be valid.

This is a work of fiction. All of the characters, names, incidents, organizations, and dialogue
in this novel are either the products of the author's imagination or are used fictitiously.

Illustrations copyright © 1989, 2007 by Eileen Christelow

Summary: Follows the adventures of Mr. Pin, a rock hopper penguin,
who leaves his home at the South Pole to be a detective in Chicago.

ISBN: 978-0-595-47247-5

Printed in the United States of America

To my parents
M.E.M.

Contents

The Mysterious Cases of
MR. PIN

Detective
PIN

1

The sky was dark. The air was cold. It had been days since Mr. Pin left his home at the South Pole to be a detective in Chicago.

A black wing pulled the bus cord at Wabash Street. The driver watched as Mr. Pin hopped out of the bus into a swarm of snowflakes.

"Mind your step," the driver said.

The door creaked shut and the bus headed west. Mr. Pin headed north.

He was at home in Chicago. It was cold.

Mr. Pin was a rock hopper penguin, mostly black and white, with long yellow plumes on both sides of his head. He wore a checked cap and a red muffler. A mysterious black bag was tucked under his wing.

Suddenly a rock hit a streetlight. Glass splintered. A black car squealed around the corner and disappeared.

Mr. Pin picked up the rock. A note was attached.

"Pay up or else," it said.

"Could be trouble," Mr. Pin said out loud, putting the rock into his black bag. "Looks like I arrived in Chicago just in time."

Just ahead was a diner — *Smiling Sally's Good Food.*

I wonder if the rock was meant for that diner, thought Mr. Pin.

The windows were iced over. A light was on, and Mr. Pin went inside. The diner was empty except for a smiling lady standing behind a curved counter.

"I'm Sally," she said.

"I'm Mr. Pin," he said, shedding his cap. "Detective Pin — reasonable rates."

"We need a detective around here," said Sally. "There's been trouble."

"Trouble?" asked Mr. Pin as he hopped up onto a stool.

"Gangsters," said Sally with a shiver. "But you don't look like you're from around here," she added, spinning a cup in her hand.

"I travel a lot, but I'm from the South Pole," said Mr. Pin, resting his beak on the counter.

"Want something cold?" asked Sally, her eyes twinkling.

"I like ice cream," said Mr. Pin. "Especially chocolate." He took off his muffler and fanned his feathers so they would dry.

"Chocolate ice cream coming right up," said Sally. "No charge."

4

"Thank you," said Mr. Pin, nodding his head sleepily.

"No reason why big cities can't have big hearts. Just call me Sally or Smiling Sally. This is my place, so I do what I want. Food's good and you meet interesting people. Where did you say you're from?"

Suddenly, with a blast of cold air, two very mean-looking customers stormed in. Sally dropped a whole tray of clean cups.

Mr. Pin sat up with a start.

Gangsters! he thought. He hopped behind a counter and grabbed a heavy rag mop. Mr. Pin was ready for trouble.

The two thugs wore shiny black shoes and trench coats with the collars pulled up to their ears. One was short. One was tall and big. The short one did the talking.

"All right, Sally," he said, "where's our money?"

"I don't have the money," said Sally. "Business has been bad since the weather's been so cold."

"Maybe you should charge more money," said the thug with a sneer as he mashed sugar cubes with a saltshaker.

"Yeah, and stop giving away so much food," said the tall one.

"I'll do the talking, Jake," snapped the short one.

"Hey, Mac, what's that?" asked Jake as Mr. Pin darted past. "Looked like a penguin."

"It's just a waiter," sniffed Mac.

"Business can't be that bad, boss. He was wearing a tuxedo," said Jake.

"Yeah," said Mac to Sally. "We want our money by midnight tomorrow or we'll blow up your diner." Mac pulled out a smelly cigar. Jake lit it and the two left to a waiting limousine.

Mr. Pin slipped out the back and watched the car pull away. It was the same black car Mr. Pin had seen when the streetlight was broken!

2

The next morning, Mr. Pin woke to the smell of warm cinnamon rolls and the sound of an elevated train rumbling past. Sally had put him up for the night on a cot in the back room.

Suddenly a little girl with curly red hair poked her head into his room and demanded, "Who are you?"

"Who are you?" asked Mr. Pin.

"I asked first," said the little girl as she came into the room and sat down.

"Very well," said Mr. Pin, studying the little girl in the blue plaid jumper. "My name is Mr. Pin, penguin detective from the South Pole."

"That's nice," said the little girl. "I'm Maggie, and I live upstairs with my Aunt Sally and two gerbils. Have you solved any crimes yet?"

"Not yet, I'm just starting. But I may have a crime to solve right here."

"Really!" said Maggie excitedly. "I think I'll be a detective, too. I don't have school today. Are you hungry?" Maggie had a way of talking all at once.

Mr. Pin was always hungry, so he quickly said yes and hopped after Maggie through the kitchen into the steamy diner.

"Hello," said Sally. "Have some nice hot cinnamon rolls."

"Thank you," said Mr. Pin as he hopped up onto a stool between two truckers. They nodded to him as they shoveled scrambled eggs into their mouths. Mr. Pin shoveled cinnamon rolls into his beak.

"Mr. Pin's from the South Pole," said Sally. "He's a penguin detective."

Mr. Pin nodded. His beak was stuck together with honey.

"This is Hank," said Maggie. "Hank delivers ice cream."

Mr. Pin's eyes lit up.

"Sally put you up for the night?" asked Hank as he elbowed the hungry penguin.

Mr. Pin nodded.

"Sally takes care of everybody," said another trucker named George. "She gives people food, puts 'em up for the night. I don't know what we'd all do without Sally and her diner."

Several truckers nodded in agreement as they bundled up in heavy coats. The diner emptied quickly as they left for work. Mr. Pin held up a sticky wing to wave good-bye.

Sally looked worried.

"It's no use," said Sally in tears as she counted the money. "We just don't have enough to pay those gangsters."

"What gangsters?" shouted Maggie.

"Jake and Mac want your aunt to pay them money by midnight or they'll blow up her diner," said Mr. Pin, wiping honey off his beak.

"That's terrible," said Maggie.

"Right," agreed Mr. Pin. "But don't worry, Sally," he said. Mr. Pin wiped Sally's eyes with a napkin. "I'll come up with a plan. At the South Pole, penguins have to stick together or they'd freeze."

Mr. Pin fanned his feathers and stared at a stack

9

of stainless steel ice cream dishes. "Freeze!" shouted Mr. Pin excitedly. "That's it. We'll freeze the gangsters."

Maggie wondered what Mr. Pin could mean by freezing gangsters and she meant to find out. Maggie followed Mr. Pin as he hurried off to the back room. Mr. Pin hopped about the room, deep in thought. All of a sudden he said, "We're going to need two chairs, two very large buckets, and lots of ice cream, preferably chocolate." Mr. Pin rummaged through his black bag and added, "I have everything else."

Maggie wrote down what Mr. Pin needed in a notebook. She liked being organized.

"How much ice cream are you going to need?" she asked.

"Enough to turn the diner into the South Pole," said Mr. Pin.

"That could be a lot," said Maggie.

"Here's the plan," said Mr. Pin. "The gangsters walk into the diner at midnight. We'll each pull a rope that is attached to a bucket of ice cream. The ice cream will fall on their heads and, presto, the thugs will turn into walking snow cones."

"What happens if the snow cones try to get away?" asked Maggie.

"I have a couple of tricks in mind," said Mr. Pin

mysteriously. "But we'll need the truckers to sur-round the diner."

"Right," said Maggie. "I'll ask Hank to bring ice cream and have the truckers here by midnight."

"Aren't the truckers in their trucks now?" asked Mr. Pin.

"I'll call them on my CB," said Maggie, running up the back stairs two at a time.

Mr. Pin hopped up after Maggie. In a small room on a desk next to a gerbil cage was a CB radio and microphone. Because there was an antenna on the roof, Maggie could talk to the truckers while they were on the road.

Maggie picked up the microphone. "Breaker 1-9, this is Orphan Annie. That's my radio name. Hank, we need ice cream fast. Preferably chocolate. Lots of it, too. It's an emergency."

"That's a roger, Annie," came the call. "But right now my truck is stuck in a snowbank and there's a blizzard on the way."

"Roger, Hank," said Maggie. "But some gangsters said they'd blow up the diner at midnight unless Sally could get them money. Sally can't, so we need ice cream for a trap, and we need trucks to surround the diner."

"We all want to help," radioed George. "But we're

11

all stuck out on the highway. Roads are closed. A semi is jackknifed. And the diner here doesn't have cinnamon rolls."

"Oh, dear!" said Maggie.

Mr. Pin hopped up on Maggie's desk and grabbed the mike. "All right, truckers. This is Detective Pin. Sally really needs your help. Now just stick together and don't give up."

Maggie manned the radio while Mr. Pin hopped down the stairs and worked on the trap. First he hammered two chairs onto the wall above the door. Then he balanced two buckets on top of the chairs. Next he tied two pieces of rope onto the handles of the buckets. When he pulled the rope, the buckets tipped down, just over the doorway.

Outside the wind howled and the snow pounded into the glass windows. Mr. Pin was worried.

"Any news?" asked Mr. Pin when Maggie came down for dinner.

"The trucks are still stuck," was all she said. She grabbed a plateful of sandwiches and hurried back upstairs to her CB.

It was almost midnight. Still no ice cream and still no truckers.

The phone rang.

"Hello," said Maggie.

12

"You got the money?" snarled Mac. He thought it was Sally.

"No problem," said Maggie.

"No tricks, lady. We'll be there at midnight," said Mac.

"Right," said Maggie.

Click.

Maggie came running down the stairs, yelling, "Mr. Pin, no ice cream, no truckers, and the gansters are coming at midnight."

Hank stormed in. "I just got out of that snowbank and I have a truckload of chocolate-chocolate-chip ice cream."

"Hurray!" shouted Maggie. "But we don't have much time."

Not minding the cold, Mr. Pin used his beak to open the ice cream and his wings to scoop it into the buckets. He dumped what was left into a huge mountain on the floor.

"Looks like home," said Mr. Pin.

"All we need now is hot fudge," said Maggie.

It was midnight.

The diner was dark.

The trap was set.

But where were the truckers?

Several black limos crunched to a stop on the newly plowed street.

The door creaked open. Black shoes glinted in the street light.

Several dark figures filled the doorway. Maggie shivered. Mac had brought his whole gang of thugs!

"Pull the ropes!" shouted Mr. Pin.

"Freeze, you thugs!" shouted Maggie. They could do little else. Gallons and gallons of ice cream avalanched onto the gangsters.

Splat. Plop. "Brrrrrrr!" they chattered.

Rope in beak, Mr. Pin tobogganed down the ice-cream mountain and tied up the sputtering, struggling thugs.

But he couldn't tie them fast enough. Some of them were getting away!

Baroomm! There was a loud rumble in the alley. A caravan of trucks had made it! The diner was surrounded.

Police lights twirled.

Officers rushed into the diner, guns drawn, but stopped cold. The gansters were tied up near a mountain of ice cream with Mr. Pin standing guard in the middle, happily preening chocolate off his feathers.

"We've been trying to catch this gang for years," said an officer named O'Malley as he handcuffed the gangsters. "How did you do it?"

"Smart detective work," said Maggie.

"Chocolate," said Mr. Pin.

16

"How much do we owe you, Detective Pin?" asked Smiling Sally. "You *will* be staying awhile."

"No charge," said Mr. Pin with a hop. "Food's good and you meet interesting people. No reason why big cities can't have big hearts."

Chicago was a lot better off with a penguin detective. But even detectives need sleep, and sleep was just ahead. Mr. Pin slipped away to the back room, where his snores were almost as loud as the trucks going home on Monroe. The South Pole was many miles away. For now, Smiling Sally's was his home.

MR. PIN
and the
Picasso Thief

1

It was bright inside the art museum. But not quiet.

Sneakers squeaked across the wood floor. A dark shadow froze under the skylight.

From the corner of his eye, Mr. Pin saw a hand reach inside its owner's coat. Bang! A balloon filled with something powdery exploded. Covered in white flour, a guard groped for his walkie-talkie. Alarms screamed.

The balloon full of flour was only a diversion. A thief was stealing a painting.

The thief was quick, but Mr. Pin was quicker. He stretched out his beak and tripped the masked robber. For a second, the mask slipped down below the nose of the green-eyed thief. He stared at Mr. Pin, not believing he had just tripped over a penguin.

More guards rushed into the room. Before the thief could be caught, he pulled up his mask and ran off, taking Picasso's famous *The Old Guitarist* with him.

Maybe there was a clue. Mr. Pin hopped over to the empty wall to find out. He dusted the museum wall with his wing and then preened his feathers. He tasted chocolate frosting! It was a clue, he

thought. But what did it mean?

Just then, his red-haired friend Maggie walked across the room with Officer O'Malley, whom Mr. Pin had first met at Smiling Sally's diner.

"Now, Mr. Pin," said O'Malley. "Can you describe the thief who tripped over your beak?"

"That painting he stole is worth a lot of money," added Maggie.

"He had green eyes and probably liked chocolate," said Mr. Pin.

"*The Old Guitarist?*" asked O'Malley.

"No," said Mr. Pin. "The thief."

"Interesting," said O'Malley, stroking his whiskers. "Did he get a look at you?"

"He knows I'm a penguin," said Mr. Pin.

"Hmmm . . ." said O'Malley. "That could be trouble. Not too many penguins go to art museums. You and Maggie could be in danger."

"Danger?" asked Maggie. "I live above Smiling Sally's diner with my Aunt Sally, two gerbils, and a CB radio. Mr. Pin lives downstairs. Truckers are around all the time. How could we be in danger?"

"Art thieves are always dangerous," said O'Malley. "I'll send Officer Jones over to the diner to protect you. Meanwhile, if you remember anything else, let me know."

"Right," said Maggie and Mr. Pin together.

23

2

Mr. Pin hopped over slush puddles and snow-banks, his red muffler flapping like a flag in the windy city. He had to hurry to keep up with Maggie.

"Why was the guitar player blue?" asked Mr. Pin.

"Because Picasso painted him during his blue period," said Maggie with authority.

"What's a blue period?" asked Mr. Pin.

"When Picasso painted everything blue," explained Maggie.

Just then Mr. Pin noticed a white panel truck following close behind them. On the side of the truck were the letters *B A K*. The other letters were splattered with slush.

The truck stopped. An elevated train rumbled overhead.

"Quick," said Mr. Pin. "Go up the stairs to the train. We're being followed!"

"What?" shouted Maggie.

"Hurry!" said Mr. Pin as he hooked a wing under her arm and pulled her up the steps.

Sneakers squeaked up the stairs. The train screeched to a stop.

As the train doors closed behind Maggie and Mr.

Pin, a man wearing a parka over a long white apron pounded on the window. Mr. Pin and Maggie crouched behind a seat and held their breath until the train left the station.

"Whew! That was close," said Maggie.

"Yes, it was," said Mr. Pin, adjusting his cap. "That man was the Picasso thief!"

Mr. Pin and Maggie rode the train back and forth for a while to be sure the Picasso thief was no longer following them. Then they got off the train, walked down the stairs and over to Smiling Sally's diner on Monroe Street.

3

Smiling Sally's was a friendly diner, open until midnight. Booths and a few tables and chairs were arranged on a black-and-white tile floor. Sally stood behind the curved counter, spinning cups in her hand and passing out hot cinnamon rolls to hungry truckers.

"Food's good and you meet interesting people," she said to a new customer.

Maggie and Mr. Pin stormed in. They waved to the truckers and hurried to Detective Pin's headquarters in the spare room behind the kitchen. Sally brought them lunch, and then they got to work.

"We know the thief has something to do with chocolate," said Mr. Pin, hopping back and forth.

"Right," said Maggie.

"We were followed by a white truck," he added.

"Right," said Maggie.

"The letters *B A K* were written on the truck," said Mr. Pin.

"Right," said Maggie.

"The first three letters in bakery are *B A K*," said Mr. Pin.

"And the man following us was wearing a white apron," added Maggie.

"The Picasso thief is a baker!" shouted Mr. Pin, hopping up and down.

"Right!" agreed Maggie. "But how do we find Mr. Green Eyes before he finds us?"

"We have to find the bakery that has the same chocolate I found on the museum wall," Mr. Pin said, chomping on a roll.

"There could be hundreds of bakeries in Chicago. How do we find the right one?" asked Maggie.

"Sometimes you have to eat to catch a thief," said Mr. Pin.

Maggie wasn't going to argue with Mr. Pin. He

had been right before, when he saved Smiling Sally's diner from being blown up by gangsters. But that was another story.

Just then a man wearing a trench coat and with a long hooked nose and black glasses opened the door. Maggie shivered.

"I'm Jones," he said. "O'Malley sent me."

"Just in time, Jones," said Mr. Pin. "We'd like to visit a few bakeries."

4

Maggie and Mr. Pin were in Jones's squad car, bouncing over potholes and mud puddles on sleet-covered streets. All of a sudden Mr. Pin ordered, "Stop the car!"

"He likes chocolate," explained Maggie to Jones.

Mr. Pin hopped out of the car and went into a German bakery filled with large tiered cakes. Mr. Pin's beak went back and forth as he surveyed the cases of pastries. Then he settled on a nice German-chocolate cake with flaky coconut in the frosting.

"Delicious" he said, hopping back into the squad car. His feathers were matted with sleet and chocolate frosting. "But I would like to try some chocolate-frosted doughnuts, please."

28

Jones sighed as he spun away from the curb. They drove from bakery to bakery, Mr. Pin sampling chocolate at every stop. Still, every time he tasted the chocolate he said, "Not quite right. One more, please."

Soon it was getting dark. Just as Mr. Pin was about to give up, he pointed with his wing and said, "Follow that truck!"

It was the white panel truck speeding straight down Michigan Avenue, past where they were parked!

"Wake up!" Maggie yelled at Jones, who had fallen asleep.

"Never mind," said Mr. Pin. "I'll drive." He leaned Jones to one side, hopped up onto his black bag, and took the wheel.

Maggie got on the radio and called O'Malley for help. Then she asked him to call Sally and tell her she was all right.

Meanwhile, Mr. Pin swerved back and forth between buses and taxis. Horns blared and buses beeped. But when people saw a penguin driving a police car, they just stopped and stared.

"Oh, no!" shouted Maggie. "I think we've lost him. All units," she said into the radio. "We need to find a white panel truck with the letters *B A K*. The driver may be the Picasso thief."

29

The radio was silent. Jones snored loudly. Then all of a sudden a voice came through.

"Spotted him just past Ohio Street." It was Hank, a trucker from Sally's diner.

"Thanks," said Maggie. "That's a roger. Over and out."

"Glad to help," said Hank.

Mr. Pin sped down Michigan Avenue to Ohio Street. There he saw the thief turn into a side street and park in front of a small bakery specializing in extra-large wedding cakes.

Mr. Pin pulled into a dark alley.

Green eyes glinted in the light as the thief got out of the truck.

"That's him," whispered Mr. Pin.

"He's going into the bakery," said Maggie.

"It has to be the bakery we're looking for," said Mr. Pin. "But where's the painting?"

"In the bakery," said Maggie.

"I have to know for sure," said Mr. Pin, hopping out of the car.

"Be careful," said Maggie. "Art thieves are dangerous."

But Mr. Pin had disappeared into the alley's shadows.

He made his way to the back door of the bakery and slowly opened it. He heard shouts inside, so

31

Mr. Pin hid in a cake box wedged between two blocks of dry ice. Frost collected on his wings, but he enjoyed the cold.

Two men were arguing.

"Leave that painting here, Borris," said one baker. He had on a tall white hat.

"It's too risky, Max," said Borris, the green-eyed baker. "That crazy penguin and the redhead are on to us. They know about the bakery. We have to move the painting."

"Too late!" shouted Mr. Pin as he slammed a freezer door into a cream-puff pastry cart. The cart skidded into Max, who toppled over a large chocolate cake.

"Hmmm. That chocolate smells familiar," said Mr. Pin, sniffing with his beak.

Outside sirens blared. Police lights twirled.

But Borris was getting away! He was carrying a very large wedding cake out the front door.

Mr. Pin grabbed his black bag and hopped after him.

As the thief started his truck, Mr. Pin opened his bag and emptied his prized rock hopper rock collection in front of the tires.

The motor whirred and the wheels spun, but the white truck wouldn't budge. The rocks had stopped the thief cold.

Squad cars skidded to a stop around the truck.

Police nabbed the thieves. They were handcuffed and loaded into a paddy wagon.

"But where's the painting?" boomed O'Malley, arriving on the scene.

"The cake!" shouted Mr. Pin, pointing to the cake in the truck.

"Oh, no," groaned Maggie. "You can't be hungry at a time like this."

Mr. Pin tasted the cake with the tip of his wing. "It's chocolate!" he said excitedly.

"Calm down, penguin," said O'Malley. "It's just a cake."

"It's a cake with a painting inside," said Mr. Pin. "The thief baked a cake around the painting. The chocolate is the same as what I found on the wall of the museum."

Sure enough, when the police scraped away a bit of the frosting on the cake, they found a carefully wrapped painting. It was Picasso's *The Old Guitarist*.

Inside the squad car, Jones woke up and asked, "Isn't that penguin full yet?" Mr. Pin wasn't. He disappeared into the bakery, hot on the trail of more chocolate. O'Malley congratulated Maggie, who insisted it was Mr. Pin who should be thanked.

Meanwhile, another police car arrived, and Smiling Sally jumped out carrying a large sack filled with cinnamon rolls.

"There you are," she said, hugging Maggie. "I knew you'd be all right, but I'm sure you're both very hungry. Where's Mr. Pin? He probably needs one of my nice hot cinnamon rolls."

At that moment Mr. Pin, another case under his belt, wobbled out the bakery door. He looked for a moment at the steaming, sugary rolls and asked, "Could we save them for breakfast?"

MR. PIN
and the
Monroe Street
Pigeon

1

It was midnight. Chicago steamed. Mr. Pin's wings stuck to the typewriter.

It had been a hot summer at Smiling Sally's diner. Mr. Pin, rock hopper penguin detective from the South Pole, was writing his memoirs. His friend Maggie was upstairs with her aunt Sally. Mr. Pin was downstairs, in his headquarters behind the kitchen.

"The sky was dark. The air was cold," typed Mr. Pin, recalling his first mystery.

Errrrrrk! Boards creaked in the diner. Mr. Pin looked up from his desk.

Errrrrrk! They creaked again. It was time to investigate. Hopping off his typing crate, Mr. Pin opened the door.

Creeeak. Thud. Someone had just gone out the back door!

Crash! Mr. Pin stumbled into a cart of coffee cups. A light switched on.

"What's going on?" It was Maggie, barefoot, red hair flying in all directions.

"I don't know," said Mr. Pin. "But someone was here, and he left a note."

Maggie picked it up. "Meet me at Buckingham Fountain before the race at noon tomorrow. I need help," Maggie read.

"Someone's in trouble," said Mr. Pin. "Memoirs can wait."

2

Monroe Street shops charged the air with smells of smoked chicken, fresh popcorn, and carry-out sushi. Everyone said hello to Maggie and Mr. Pin as they walked toward Buckingham Fountain. Mr. Pin bought a *Tribune* and flipped to the city news.

"Another day of politics," said Mr. Pin.

Meanwhile, Maggie was looking at chocolate pigeons in the window of a chicken store.

"Why would a chicken shop sell chocolate pigeons?" said Mr. Pin.

"I don't know," said Maggie. "And I wonder where Pete the chicken man is."

"He's missing," said his wife Florrie, who had just come out of the store.

"Who's missing?" asked Mr. Pin, looking up from his papers.

"The chicken man," said Maggie.

"Pete put the trash in a grocery cart and went

outside to dump it. He hasn't been back since," said Florrie. "I'm beginning to get worried."

"What was he wearing?" asked Mr. Pin.

"A big, baggy coat," said Florrie.

"We're on another case," said Mr. Pin. "But we'll keep an eye out for him."

"Now there are two cases to solve," said Maggie as they continued east on Monroe. "The chicken man is missing and someone is in trouble at Buckingham Fountain."

There was little time to talk. Soon it would be noon and a ten-kilometer race was about to start in Grant Park.

The city seared. Waves of heat curled from the sidewalk. Most penguins would die in this weather. But Mr. Pin was no ordinary penguin.

The two detectives rushed past the Art Institute, the scene of another mystery. Someone had stolen a famous Picasso. But that was another story.

Maggie and Mr. Pin hurried through Grant Park to Buckingham Fountain. Numbered runners stretched, drank Gatorade, and talked about the heat.

Just ahead a homeless lady sat on a bench feeding the pigeons. A grocery cart filled with her possessions was parked next to her. The pigeons flocked like children listening to a story. Mr. Pin marveled that homeless people fed pigeons.

Big cities can have big hearts, he thought.

"I wonder whom we're meeting before the race," said Maggie.

"Hmmmm," said Mr. Pin calmly. "It isn't *before* the race anymore. The race is *starting*." A wall of runners raced past Maggie and Mr. Pin. The two detectives scrambled onto the fountain.

"Look out!" shouted Maggie.

The homeless lady was steering her cart wildly through the runners toward Maggie and Mr. Pin. A runner who did not look like the other runners was chasing the homeless lady. He had a number. But he was wearing shiny black shoes.

The runner caught the homeless lady and snatched a box that was hidden in her cart. Maggie fumed. How could someone steal from a homeless person?

The homeless lady wrenched the box out of the runner's hands and tossed it to Maggie. Maggie caught the box but fell backward into the fountain. Mr. Pin hopped in and grabbed the box, just before it hit the water. He quickly swam to the other side. The thief snarled at Mr. Pin, but the wall of runners forced him away from the fountain.

The homeless lady had vanished.

Now Maggie and Mr. Pin had a mysterious box from a mysterious lady who was chased by a runner

who wasn't a runner.

"That wasn't a runner," said Maggie.

"I know," said Mr. Pin. "And that wasn't a home-less lady."

"Who was it?" asked Maggie, astonished.

"*That* was the chicken man."

"How do you know?" asked Maggie.

"There was a chicken on the side of his grocery cart," said Mr. Pin.

"No wonder Pete the chicken man was missing. He wasn't there, because he was here." Maggie was very logical.

"Right," said Mr. Pin, who understood Maggie's logic.

"We have to find him," said Maggie.

"And we have to find out what's in this box," said Mr. Pin.

3

"Aunt Sally is going to worry," said Maggie, skipping after her penguin friend. Sally always worried when they missed a meal.

"Right," said Mr. Pin, hopping over potholes. His red beak darted through the crowd of lunchtime shoppers. Overhead, an elevated train screeched to a stop. Maggie and Mr. Pin burst into Smiling Sally's diner.

Inside the diner there was a crush of hungry truckers. Sally was busy flipping burgers and pouring cool lemonade. Sally loved feeding people, especially Maggie and Mr. Pin.

"You're all right," said Sally to Mr. Pin. With a wide smile, she handed him a tall lemonade. Sally had a smile that sang.

"I don't know too many penguins who can handle this heat," said the trucker named Hank, whisking away sweat.

"I don't know too many penguins," said a confused man who was delivering ice.

"You don't know Mr. Pin," said Hank. "Mr. Pin is a detective. He's been here since he saved Sally from a gang of gangsters."

"That's right," said Sally. "Now what'll it be, Maggie dear. You had me a bit worried when you were late for lunch."

But Maggie was worried about the chicken man. She didn't want the trail to get cold while they sat in the steamy diner.

Mr. Pin tucked cinnamon rolls, grilled-cheese sandwiches, and lemonade under his wing and steered Maggie to the back room.

Maggie spread the food out on Mr. Pin's desk.

46

Meanwhile, Mr. Pin made short work of the tape and string around the homeless lady's mysterious box.

Quickly, Maggie pulled shreds of paper from the box. Underneath there was more paper and finally a roll of cotton.

"It's a chocolate pigeon!" shouted Maggie.

"It doesn't smell right," said Mr. Pin. "It's not chocolate."

"Then what is it?" asked Maggie.

"Clay," said Mr. Pin.

"If it's not chocolate, then why would the homeless lady who's really the chicken man give us a clay pigeon that looks like a chocolate pigeon when he's being chased by a runner who isn't a runner?" Maggie had a way of talking all at once.

"I don't know," said Mr. Pin, "but I'm going to find out."

"And where," asked Maggie, "did the chicken man go?"

Moments later Mr. Pin and Maggie were hot on the trail of the chicken man. First stop was the chicken shop on Monroe.

Florrie, the chicken man's wife, was wringing her hands.

"He's here, but I don't know what's wrong with him," she cried. "Ever since his uncle George died, Pete's been so . . . strange."

47

Maggie and Mr. Pin went to the back room, where Pete the chicken man sat on a stool, shaking.

"Why did you give us a clay pigeon?" asked Mr. Pin.

"And why did you meet us at the park?" asked Maggie.

"I had no choice. Someone was following me," said Pete. "So I disguised myself as a homeless lady. I always liked pigeons. My uncle George used to take me to the park to feed them. He gave me a clay pigeon just before he died. He said it could be very valuable. He also gave me hundreds of chocolate pigeons from his chocolate shop in Indiana."

Mr. Pin looked at the clay pigeon and wondered how it could be valuable. Chocolate pigeons seemed more artistic. . . . Maybe it was a clue.

"Uncle George said we could use this pigeon to help homeless people," said Pete. "We need to find out why this bird is valuable before we can help anyone. Uncle George never had a chance to tell me."

"Maybe it's priceless art," said Maggie.

"I don't know," said Pete. "But I do know someone else wants it."

"The runner in the park," said Mr. Pin. "We'll set a trap and bait it with a chocolate pigeon. It may be dangerous. Are you willing to take a chance?"

48

"Yes," said Pete.

"Now here's the trap," explained Mr. Pin. "Wrap up a chocolate pigeon in a box like the one you gave us. Bring it to the diner tonight. Hopefully the runner will trail you to Smiling Sally's."

"All right," said Pete, still shaking. "I'll do it. Thanks —"

But before Pete could finish thanking them, Mr. Pin and Maggie had disappeared.

4

Smiling Sally's diner simmered in the evening heat. Sally was busy in the alley passing out free food to homeless people. Mr. Pin and Maggie waited inside. Pete's clay pigeon was safely hidden in Mr. Pin's black bag, which he kept in the back room.

A slow ceiling fan cranked in the sweltering silence.

The diner was empty when Pete the chicken man approached the door. Suddenly he tripped on a black shiny foot and threw his box into the air. For the second time that day, Mr. Pin caught the box just in time.

From a shadow came the shiny-shoed runner, a skinny man wearing a knit cap.

49

Pete froze.

"I want that pigeon," growled the runner.

"What's so great about a clay pigeon," asked Mr. Pin, stepping toward the door.

"It's not the bird," sneered the skinny man. "It's the jewels."

Maggie's eyes popped.

Pete plopped onto a stool.

"What jewels?" probed Mr. Pin, his mind racing.

"The jewels in the bird. I helped George make chocolate pigeons in Indiana. He ran the shop. I stirred the vats. One day he said he hid his grandmother's jewels in a clay pigeon. He said he was giving them to his nephew. Now I want that pigeon."

Mr. Pin had an idea. "You can have the pigeon," he said. "But this is the wrong one. The real pigeon is in the back room.

Maggie couldn't believe her ears.

Pete was stunned. Mr. Pin was going to give the jewels to a crook. The homeless people would never get warm clothes and food to eat.

Mr. Pin hopped off to get his black bag. When he returned, he gave the thief the clay bird and had him promise never to bother Pete again.

Pete buried his head in his hands while the runner who was not a runner snickered and cackled out the door.

But Mr. Pin had a plan.

"Quick," he said. "Back to the chicken shop. One of the Monroe Street chocolate pigeons is the real thing. That clay bird is a fake."

"How do you know?" asked Maggie.

"Because Uncle George did not tell Pete that the pigeon *was* valuable. He said it *could* be valuable," explained Mr. Pin. "Uncle George wanted people to believe the jewels were in the clay pigeon. That way, Pete would always have the jewels safe in a chocolate bird."

"Why was a chocolate bird safer than a clay bird?" asked Maggie.

"Because Uncle George had hundreds of chocolate pigeons. Think of all the hundreds of hiding places to confuse a thief. Besides, why would anyone hide jewels in a clay pigeon when he had a chocolate pigeon?"

"You're right," said Pete, dabbing his eyes. "He loved chocolate."

"A great man," said Mr. Pin, "who knew his chocolate and wanted to help the homeless."

Maggie, Pete, and Mr. Pin raced back to the chicken shop. They chopped up several chocolate birds and finally found the glittering jewels. A siren wailed in the distance.

"I called the police," said Mr. Pin, "while I was

in back getting the box."

"Good thinking," said Maggie.

"Thanks," said Pete.

"I don't think that scoundrel will be bothering any of us again," said Maggie. "Right, Mr. Pin?"

But Mr. Pin didn't answer. He was happily preening chocolate from his wing . . . and thinking that his memoirs would be one chapter longer.

978-0-595-47247-5
0-595-47247-8

LaVergne, TN USA
23 May 2010
183566LV00001B/22/A